Fireman Ken

Fireman Ken

Written by Ellen Tarlow

Illustrated by Terry Widener

SCHOLASTIC INC.

New York   Toronto   London   Auckland   Sydney
Mexico City   New Delhi   Hong Kong   Buenos Aires

Ken is in bed.

Ken naps.

Buzz!

Ken is up.

Ken gets his red hat.

Ken runs.

Ken hops on.

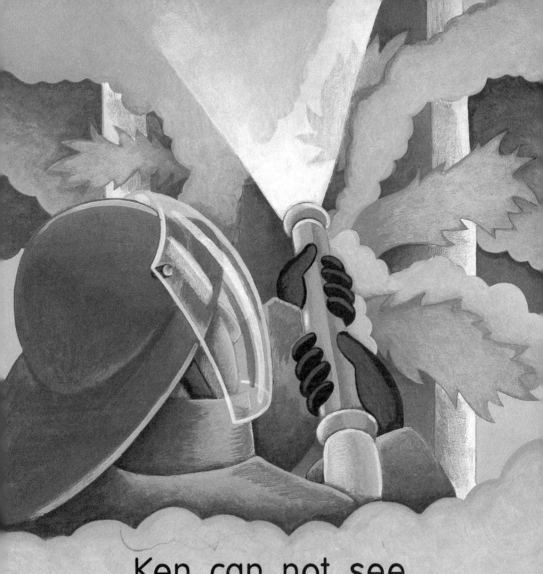

Ken can not see.
It is hot.

It is wet, wet, wet.
The fire is out.

But a dog is on top!
Ken gets a net.

Ken did his job.
Ken gets a kiss.
Ken gets a hug.

Ken naps.
All is well.
Thank you, Ken!

ISBN-13: 978-0-545-06958-8
ISBN-10: 0-545-06958-0

12 11 10 9 8 7 6 5 4 3   8 9 10 11 12 13/0

Printed in the U.S.A.   23

This edition first printing, March 2008